Bungalo Books

Written and Illustrated by John Bianchi
Copyright 1996 by Bungalo Books

Canadian Cataloguing in Publication Data

Bianchi, John
   Welcome back to Pokeweed Public School

ISBN 0-921285-45-0 (bound)   ISBN 0-921285-44-2 (pbk.)

I. Title

PS8553.I26W44 1996   jC813'.54   C96-900201-7
PZ7.B47126We 1996

Published in Canada by:
Bungalo Books
Ste.100
17 Elk Court
Kingston, Ontario
K7M 7A4

Co-published in U.S.A. by:
Firefly Books (U.S.) Inc.
Ellicott Station
P.O. Box 1338
Buffalo, New York
14205

Welcome Back to Pokeweed Public School

Written & Illustrated by
John Bianchi

The week before school started, Mom took me down to Eggberty's General Store. She bought me some new jeans, a new shirt and a pair of new running shoes. Then she let me pick out some really cool school supplies.

I spent the next two days organizing my backpack until everything was just right.

Finally, the big day arrived. As always, my best friend Melody had saved me a seat on the bus — right up front. It didn't take long to slip into our old bus-riding routine:

When we drove under the bridge near Lost Worm Lake, everyone yelled, "Duck your head!"

When we crossed the railroad tracks, we all lifted our feet and shouted, "Make a wish!"

And when the bus ran over a pothole, Bus Driver Bernie called, "Speed bump!" Everyone laughed as we bounced high into the air.

We passed Mrs. Henten's turkey ranch, headed down Whispering Pines Side Road and rolled into the parking lot at Pokeweed Public School right on time.

When we got to class, good old Ms. Mudwortz, our teacher, introduced the new students to the class. Buwocka was from Africa, and Bruce was from Australia. They needed the big globe to show us where they used to live.

Then we all headed down to the official opening-day ceremony.

Principal Slugmeyer had some very special announcements about all the new things at Pokeweed Public School.

There were new computers in the new computer lab; a fancy new fire-alarm system complete with automatic sprinklers; special new locks on all the doors; and a big new computer in his office that controlled everything. While we were on summer vacation, Pokeweed Public School had become a very "high-tech" kind of place.

After the announcements, we were given a tour of the new computer lab. While Ms. Mudwortz helped Buwocka and Bruce send E-mail letters to their friends back home, Principal Slugmeyer taught the rest of us how to use the new computers. Hardly anyone had a problem.

Before we left the computer lab, Principal Slugmeyer warned us to be ready for a fire drill at any time. Sure enough, right in the middle of lunch, the alarm started ringing.

We all lined up, filed down the hall and headed straight out the front door. The system performed without a flaw . . . except for the sprinklers.

When it was time for us to head back into the school, we discovered a small problem — the wet computer had locked all the new locks on all the old doors. We were stuck outside!

Principal Slugmeyer waded around his desk, plugging and unplugging different combinations of cables. Nothing seemed to work.

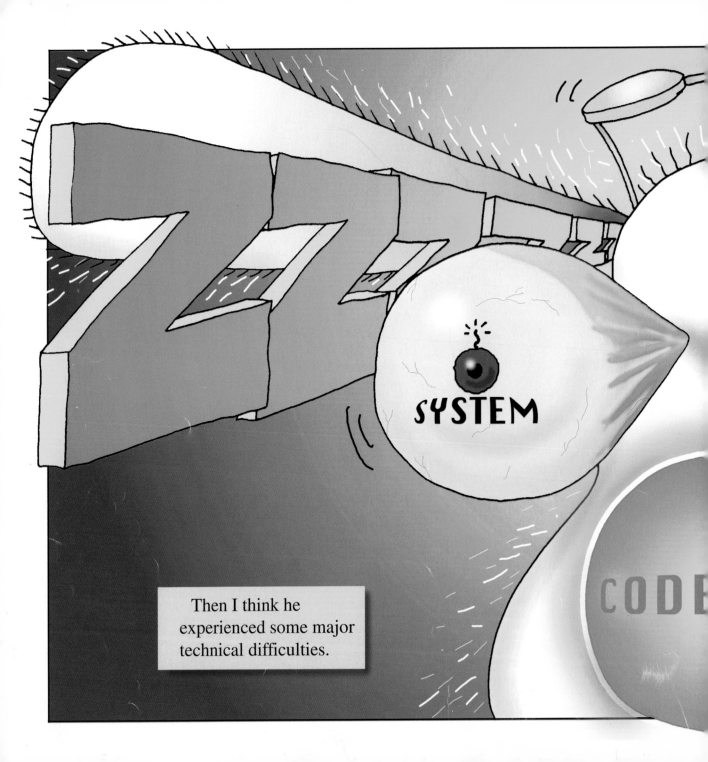

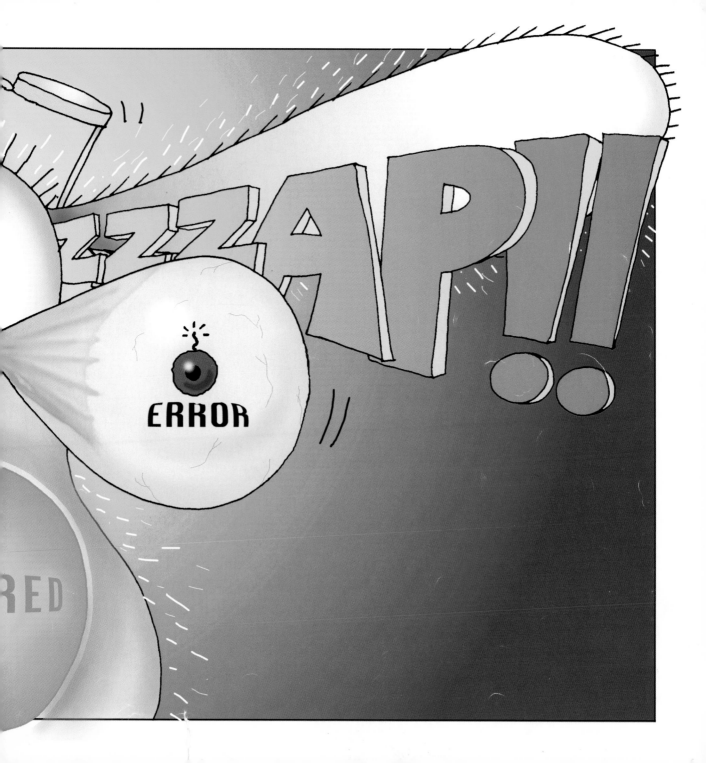

That was when good old Ms. Mudwortz calmly took control of the whole situation. First, she reached through Principal Slugmeyer's office window and pulled out all the plugs on the new computer. That unlocked the doors. Then she went inside and handed Principal Slugmeyer a towel and announced that we would do something new on our first day this year — we were going to go on a field trip to look for the signs of fall.

Ms. Mudwortz and Principal Slugmeyer lined us all up and left Custodian Cathy to fix the computer and dry out the school.

On our walk, we all noticed different things. Billy told us he knew fall was coming when the Pokeweed Grizzlies started practising for their Sunday-afternoon football games. Melody and I saw birds flying south to escape winter. And everyone noticed that the trees were changing colour.

We were so well behaved that Ms. Mudwortz decided to stop at the Big Scoop Ice Cream Factory. Her Cousin Camilla worked there and took us on a tour of the whole place. We looked at all the equipment and watched the staff mix up a new batch of ice cream. Camilla even asked us to suggest names for the newest fall flavours. I thought Melody's "Pumpkin Paradise" sounded the best.

During question time, Principal Slugmeyer asked whether they ever used computers to make their jobs easier. Camilla just laughed and said that new computers might not be good at making old-fashioned ice cream.

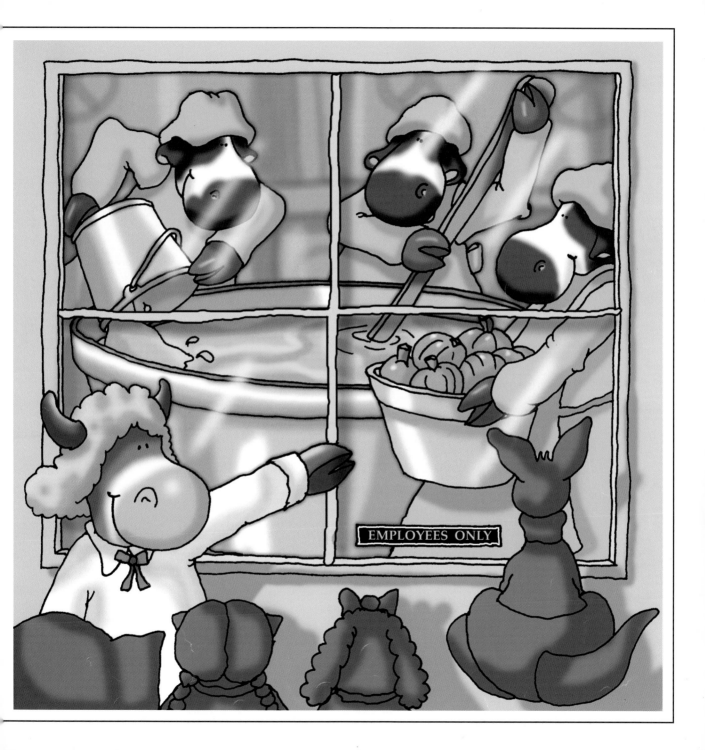

But the best part was when we stopped at the dairy bar. Melody ordered a scoop of Mint Corn-Chip ice cream in a waffle cone, and I had an extra-large Hay Freezie.

And we didn't even need any money, because Ms. Mudwortz asked Principal Slugmeyer to show us how his new electronic bank card could pay for everything.

By the time we got back to the school, Custodian Cathy had dried out the new computer and mopped up the whole building.

Before we knew it, our first day was over and it was time to head for home. As we rode the bus, Melody and I agreed that even though there were lots of new things at school, the best part of going back was being with all our old friends and teachers.

And this year, things seemed to be off to a great old start at Pokeweed Public School.

The Author

John Bianchi is a cartoonist, illustrator and author who divides his time between his studio in Arizona's Sonoran Desert, where he lives with his family, and Bungalo World Headquarters in eastern Ontario. A well-known magazine illustrator in Canada and the United States, he co-founded Bungalo Books in 1986 and has more than twenty children's books to his credit.